Timothy Kavanagh
107 Wisteria Lane
Mitford

We — or at least I — shall not be able to adore God on the highest occasions if we have learned no habit of doing so on the lowest. At best, our faith and reason will tell us that He is adorable, but we shall not have found Him so, not have "tasted and seen." Any patch of sunlight in a wood will show you something about the sun which you could never get from reading books on astronomy. These pure and spontaneous pleasures are "patches of godlight" in the woods of experience.

C. S. Lewis,
Letters to Malcolm: Chiefly on Prayer

He who refreshes others will himself be refreshed.

— Proverbs 11:25

People may doubt what you say, but they believe what you do.

— Wayside pulpit message

There is nothing that makes us love someone so much as praying for them.

— William Law

One man with beliefs is equal to a thousand with only interests.

— John Stuart Mill

Enough, if something from our
hands have power, to live
and act and serve the future
hour.
— Wordsworth

How does the meadow flower its
    bloom unfold?
Because the lovely little flower is
    free
Down to its root, and in that
    freedom, bold.
— Wordsworth

The soft blue sky did never melt
Into his heart; he never felt
the witchery of the soft blue sky!
— Wordsworth

If you read history you will find
that the Christians who diid most
for the present world were those
who thought most of the next. The
apostles themselves, who set out on
foot to convert the Roman Empire,
the great men who buiilt up the
Middle Ages, the English evangeli-
cals ᴋwho abolished the slave trade,
all left theiir mark on earth,
precisely because their minds were
occupied with Heaven. It is since
Christians have largely ceased to
thiink of the other world that they
have become so ineffective iin this
one. Aim at Heaven and you will get
 earth "Thrown in." Aim at earth and
you will get neither.

                    --C. S. Lewis

None can love freedom heartily
but good men; the rest love not
freedom, but license.
— Milton

A good question for an atheist
is to serve him a fine dinner,
& then ask if he believes there
is a cook.

"For the Benefit of Clergy,"
as seen in The Anglican Digest

Thou wilt keep him in perfect
peace whose mind is stayed
on thee . . .
— Isaiah 26:3

We must remember that hatred is like acid. It does more damage to the vessel in which it is stored than to the object on which it is poured.

Ann Landers column

It is wonderful how much may be done if we are always doing.

Thomas Jefferson

...to reach the port of heaven, we must sail sometimes with the wind and sometimes against it — but we must sail, and not drift, nor lie at anchor.

Oliver Wendell Holmes

Ring the bells that still can ring,
Forget your perfect offering.
There is a crack in everything.
That's how the light gets in.

— Leonard Cohen

God does not give us overcoming
life; He gives life as we overcome. The strain is the strength.
If there is no strain there is
no strength. Are you asking
God to give you life and liberty
and joy? He cannot, unless
you will accept the strain.
Immediately you face the
strain, you will get the
strength.
                    Oswald Chambers,
          "My Utmost for His Highest"

God never gives strength for
tomorrow or the next hour,
but only for the strain of the
minute.
                    Ibid.

It is not a question of our
equipment but of our poverty,
not of what we bring with
us, but of what God puts into
us.

Ibid.

The main thing about Christianity is not the work we do,
but the relationship we maintain and the atmosphere
produced by that relationship.
That is all God asks us to look
after, and it is the one thing
that is being continually
assailed.

Ibid.

Bottom line

The Bible without the Holy Spirit
is a sundial by moonlight.

Dwight L. Moody, 1837—1899

When such as I cast out remorse
So great a sweetness flows into
the breast ...

W. B. Yeats

The Lord sends no one away
empty except those who are
full of themselves.

Dwight L. Moody

As is our confidence, so is our
capacity.

William Hazlitt

Lord, make me see thy glory in
every place.

Michelangelo

The days that make us happy
make us wise.

John Masefield

I long to accomplish a great
and noble task, but it is my
chief duty to accomplish
small tasks as if they were
great and noble.

Helen Keller

I have been suspected of being
what is called a fundamentalist.
That is because I never regard
any narrative as unhistorical
simply on the ground that it
includes the miraculous.

C. S. Lewis, The Joyful Christian

With my mother's death, all
settled happiness, all that was
tranquil and reliable, disappeared
from my life. There was to be
much fun, many pleasures,
many stabs of Joy; but no more
of the old security. It was
sea and islands, now; the
great continent had sunk like
Atlantis...

Ibid.

In commanding us to glorify Him, God is inviting us to enjoy Him.

Ibid.

Laziness means more work in the long run.

Ibid.

The great difficulty is to get modern audiences to realize that you are preaching Christianity solely and simply because you happen to think it true; they always suppose you are preaching it because you like it or think it good for society or something of that sort...

Ibid.

The Christian way is diiferent: harder, and easier. Christ says, "Give me All. I don't want so much of your time and so much of your money and so much of your work: I want You.. . No half-measures are any good. i don't want to cut off a branch here and a branch there, I want to have the whole tree down . . . Hand over the whole natural l self, all the desires whiich you think innocent as well as the ones you thiink wicked--the whole outfit. I will give you a new self instead. I will give you Myself: my own will shall become yours."

--C. S. Lewis, <u>The Joyful Christian</u>

When I get a little money I
buy books, and if any is left
I buy food and clothes.

Erasmus

I have a dream that my
four little children will one
day live in a nation where
they will not be judged by the
color of their skin but by the
content of their character.

Martin Luther King, Jr.

Civilization and violence are
antithetical concepts.

Martin Luther King, Jr.,
Nobel Prize acceptance speech, '64

Faith is the substance of things hoped for, the evidence of things not seen.

Hebrews 11:1

How desperately difficult it is to be honest with oneself. It is much easier to be honest with other people.

Edward White Benson,
Archbishop of Canterbury

I have been tortured with longing to believe ... and the yearning grows stronger the more cogent the intellectual difficulties stand in the way.

Fyodor Dostoyevsky

Remember Morris L.

If a man cannot be a Christian
where he is, he cannot be a
Christian anywhere.

Henry Ward Beecher

God strengthens me to bear myself
That heaviest weight of all to bear
inalienable weight of care.

Christina Rossetti

It is as absurd to pretend that
one cannot love the same
woman always, as to pretend
that a good artist needs several
violins to execute a piece of
music.

Honoré de Balzac

We are called to be salt. Give them salt! It will lead them to drink.

Overheard at a house blessing

A good marriage is that in which each appoints the other guardian of his solitude.

Rainer Maria Rilke

He prayed me into a good frame of mind, and if he had stopped there, it would have been very well; but he prayed me out of it again by keeping on.

George Whitefield

Do all the good you can
By all the means you can
In all the ways you can
In all the places you can
To all the people you can
As long as ever you can.

John Wesley

Once in seven years I burn all
my sermons for it is a shame
if I cannot write better sermons
now than I did seven years ago.

J. Wesley

A comprehended God is no
God at all.

Gerhard Tersteegen

Do not turn to prayer hoping
to enjoy spiritual delights;
rather come to prayer totally
content to receive nothing or to
receive great blessing from God's
hand, whichever should be
your heavenly father's will
for you at that time.

Madame Jeanne Guyon, 1648—1717

Preaching should break a hard
heart and heal a broken one.

John Newton,
wrote "Amazing Grace"

When you meditate, imagine that Jesus Christ in person is about to talk to you about the most important thing in the world. Give him your complete attention. *Yes!*

François Fénelon, Archbishop of Cambrai, 1651–1715

Talents are best nurtured in solitude: character is best formed in the stormy billows of the world.

Goethe

If thou could'st empty
all thyself of self
Like to a shell dishabited
Then might He find thee
On the ocean's shelf
And say— this is not dead—
And fill thee with Himself
Instead.

T. E. Brown

Sweet joy but two days old
Sweet joy I call thee
Thou dost smile
I sing the while
Sweet joy befall thee.

William Blake

We are not citizens of this world
trying to make our way to heaven; we
are citizens of heaven trying to make
our way through thiis world. That rad-
ical Christian insight can be life-
changing. We are not to live so as
to earn God's love, inherit heaven,
and purchase our salvation. All those
are giiven to us as gifts; gifts
bought by Jesus on the cross and
handed over to us. We are to live as
God's redeemed, as heirs of heaven,
and as citizens of another land: the
Kingdom of God . .. We liive as those
who are on a journey home; a home we
know will have the lights on and the
door open and our Father waiting for
us when we arrive. That means iin all
adversity our worship of God is joyful, our life is hopeful, our future
is secure. There is nothing we can
lose on earth that can rob us of the
treasures God has given us and will
give us.

The Laddisfarne, via The Anglican

Digest

Let the Stable Yes! Still Astonish

Let the stable still astonish:
Straw—dirt floor, dull eyes,
Dusty flanks of donkeys, oxen;
Crumbling, crooked walls;
No bed to carry that pain,
And then, the child,
Rag-wrapped, laid to cry
In a trough.
Who would have chosen this?
Who would have said: "Yes,
Let the God of all the heavens
     and earth
Be born here, in this place"?

Who but the same God
Who stands in the darker, fouler
    rooms
of our hearts
and says, "Yes,
let the God of Heaven and Earth
be born here—
in this place."

Leslie Leyland Fields

Send to Stuart

Because it is sure of its beauty,
the rose makes terrible demands
on us.

Alain Meilland,
American rose breeder, 20th century

Deep in their roots, all flowers
keep the light.

Theodore Roethke, 1908—1963

A flash of dew, a bee or
two,
A breeze
A caper in the trees,
And I'm a rose!

Em. Dickinson, 1830—1886

In a garden suspended in time,
   my mother sits in a redwood
   chair
light fills the sky, the folds of
   her dress, the roses tangled
   beside her . . .

   Mark Strand, American poet

In many ways doth the full
   heart reveal
The presence of the love it
   would conceal.

   from Poems Written in Later Life,
                        Coleridge

Prayer does not fit us for
the greater work; prayer is the
greater work.

   Oswald Chambers

Keep a clear eye toward life's end. Do not forget your purpose and destiny as God's creature. What you are in His sight is what you are and nothing more.

Remember that when you leave this earth, you can take nothing that you have received ...but only what you have given; a full heart enriched by honest service, love, sacrifice and courage.

Francis of Assisi,
"Letters to Rulers of People"

The fool wonders, the wise man asks.

Disraeli

To a poet, nothing is useless.

Samuel Johnson

Many things I have tried to grasp, and have lost. That which I have placed in God's hands I still have.

— Martin Luther

When you find yourself facing an
issue in your life, the purpose or
reason or good thing that might come
out of it being completely hidden
from you--what do you do? Do you
worry and fret, become preoccupied
wiith the problem? Do you ignore it
or avoid it? Do you complain about
it, do you want to run away from it?
Or do you see iit as a situation in
 which you might be able to experience
the power and grace of God at work?
Do you watch for the work of God
that iis to be done in this situation?
--Fr. John Yates, Falls Church

write John

The true test of civilization is not the census, nor the size of the cities, nor the crops — no, but the kind of man the country turns out.

Emerson

Love one another with mutual affection; outdo one another in showing honor.

Romans 12:10

Preach "Outdo"

What lies behind us and what lies before us are tiny matters compared to what lies within us.

Ralph Waldo Emerson

Never has the world had a greater need for love than in our day. People are hungry for love. We don't have time to stop and smile at each other. We are all in such a hurry! Pray. Ask for the necessary grace. Pray to be able to understand how much Jesus loved us, so that you can love others.

Mother Teresa

For us, with the rule of right and wrong given us by Christ, there is nothing for which we have no standard.

Leo Tolstoy

The shepherds sing; and shall I
    silent be?
My God, no hymn for thee?
My soul's a shepherd too; a
    flock it feeds
Of thoughts, and words, and
    deeds.
The pasture is Thy Word; the
    streams, Thy Grace
Enriching all the place
Shepherd and flock shall sing,
    and all my powers
Out-sing the daylight hours.

— George Herbert, 1593—1633

Welcome! all Wonders in one sight!
Eternity shut in a span,
Summer in winter, day in night,
Heaven in earth, and God in man.
Great little one! whose all—
    embracing birth
Lifts earth to heaven, stoops
    heav'n to earth!

    Richard Crashaw (1613?—1649)

Goodness is the only investment
that never fails.

        Henry David Thoreau

The only thing necessary for
the triumph of evil is for
good men to do nothing.
                        Edmund Burke

Be imitators of God . . . and
live a life of love.
                        Ephesians 5:1

And I smiled to think God's
    greatness flowed round
        our incompleteness,
Round our restlessness His
    rest . . .

            "Rhyme of the Duchess,"
            E. B. Browning

I don't know whether nice people tend to grow roses, or growing roses makes people nice.

Roland A. Browne, 1939–

Where you tend a rose, my lad, a thistle cannot grow.

Frances Hodgson Burnett, 1859–1924

Exuberance is beauty.

William Blake

Excerpts from Oswald Chambers,
"My Utmost for His Highest,"
from his lectures at Clapham,
1911-1915, and talks at Zeitoun,
Egypt, 1915-1917

(Fretting) always ends iin sin.
We imagine that a little anxiety
and worry are an indication of
how really wise we are; it is
much more an indication of how
really wicked we are. Fretting
springs from a determination to
get our own way. Our Lord never
worried and He was never anxious,
because He was not out to realize His own ideas; He was out
to realize God's ideas.

God gives us the vision, then
He takes us down to the valley
to batter us into the shape of
the vision, and iit is in the
valley that so many of us
faint and give way. Every vision
will be made real if we will
have patience . . . God has to
take us into the valley, and
put us through fires and floods.
. . .until we get to the place
where He can trust uswith the
veritable reality . . . Let Him

*Note: The Veritable
reality*

put you on His wheel and whirl
you as He likes, and as sure as
God is God and you are you, you
will turn out exactly in accord-
ance with the vision.

    . . . all noble things are dif-
ficult

    Let me say I believe God will
supply all my need, and then let
me run dry, with no outlook, and
see whether I will go through
the trial of faith, or whether
i will sink back to something
lower.

    Faith must be tested, because
iit can be turned into a personal possession only through con-
flict . . . The final thing is
confidence in Jesus. believe
steadfastly on Him and all you
come up against will develop
your faith . . .Faith is unutter-
able trust in God, trust which
never dreams that He will not
stand by us.

    You never can measure what God
will do through you iif you are
rightly related to Jesus Christ.
Keep your relationship right with

Him, then whatever circum-
stances you are in, and who-
ever you meet day by day, He
is pouring rivers of living
water through you, and it
is of His mercy that He does
not let you know it . . .It is
the work that G od does through
us that counts, not what we do
for Him. *Bottom line again!*

God never coerces us. In one
mood we wish He would make us
do the thing, and in another
mood we wish He would leave us
al one. Whenever God's will is
iin the ascendant, all compul-
sion is gone. When we choose
deliberately to obey Him, then
He will tax the remotest star
and the last grain of sand to
assist us with all His almighty
power.

The surf that distresses the
ordinary swimmer produces in
the surf-rider the super-joy
of going straight through it.

A river is victoriously per-
sistent, it overcomes all bar-
riers. For a while it goes
steadily on its course, then
it comes to an obstacle and
for a while iit is balked,

but it soon makes a pathway
round the obstacle . . .
You can see God using some lives,
but into your life an obstacle
has come and you do not seem to
be of any use. Keep paying attention to the Source, and God
will either take you round (it)
or remove iit . ..Never get
your eyes on the obstacle or on
the difficulty . . .

The height of the mountaintop
is measured by the drab drudgery
of the valley . . *Key very key*

If you have become bitter and
sour, it is because when God gave
you a blessing you clutched it
for yourself . . . If you are
always taking blessings to yourself and never learn to pour out
anything unto the Lord, other
people do not get their horizon
enlarged through you.

*Sermon
May
16?*

The call of God is like the
call of the sea, no one hears
iit but the one who has the
nature of the sea in him.

We are not here to prove God
answers prayer; we are here to
be living monuments of God's
grace . . . When a prayer seems
to be unanswered, beware of trying to fix the blame on someone
else. That is always a snare . ..
You will find there is a reason
whiich is a deep instruction to
you . . . not to anyone else.

Waiting for the vision that
tarries is the test of our
loyalty to God.

You always know when the
vision isof God because of
the inspiration that comes
with it; things come wiith
largeness and tonic to the
life because everything is
energized by God.

Let God have perfect liberty
when you speak. Before God's
message can liberate other
souls, the liberation must be
real in you. Gather your mater-
ial, and set it alight when
you speak.

Set it alight!

How little people know who
think that holiness is dull...
When one meets the real thing,
it's irresistible.

C. S. Lewis

Doxología

A Dios, el Padre celestial,
Al Hijo, nuestro Redentor,
Y al Eternal Consolador,
Unidos, todos alabad.

(To see it written in another
language shakes me from a
kind of sleep. Consolador! El
Padre celestial! A Dios! Yes,
and yes again!)

A thankful heart is not only
the greatest virtue, but the
parent of all other virtues.

Cicero in Oratio Pro Cnaeo Plancio, XXXiii

Pride slays thanksgiving, but
an humble mind is the soil
out of which thanks naturally
grow. A proud man is seldom
a grateful man, for he never
thinks he gets as much as he
deserves.

Henry Ward Beecher

The worship most acceptable to
God comes from a thankful
and cheerful heart.

Plutarch, c. A.D. 100

Rejoice with those who rejoice
and weep with those who
weep.

Romans 12:15

Some people complain that God
put thorns on roses, while
others praise Him for putting
roses on thorns.

Anon.

Were there no God, we would
be in this glorious world with
grateful hearts, and no one to
thank.

Christina Rossetti, 1830—1894

May Heaven protect the zeal
of my heart.

—from a Mozart chorale?

O Lord, that lends me life,
lend me a heart replete with
thankfulness.
    Shakespeare, Henry VI, part 2

Thou has given me so
much...Give me one thing
more, a grateful heart.
        George Herbert, 1593—1633

In everything give thanks.
        St. Paul, I Thessalonians 5:18

Be thankful for the smallest blessing, and you will receive greater. Value the least gifts no less than the greatest, and simple graces as especial favors. If you remember the dignity of the Giver, no gift will seem small or mean, for nothing can be valueless that is given by the most high God.

Thomas à Kempis, 1380–1471

There is a God-shaped vacuum in the heart of every person and it can never be filled by any created thing. It can only be filled by God, made known through Jesus Christ.

Blaise Pascal — Hardly older than Dooley when he penned this

He ate and drank the precious
    words,
His spirit grew robust;
He knew no more that he was
    poor,
Nor that his frame was dust.
He danced along the dingy
    days,
And this bequest of wings
Was but a book. What liberty
A loosened spirit brings!

Emily Dickinson

Cultivate my heart, Lord, so I may catch every word that falls from heaven—every syllable of encouragement, every sentence of rebuke, every paragraph of instruction, every page of warning. Help me to catch these words as the soft, fertile soil catches seeds.

Ken Gire

Cheerfulness and contentment are great beautifiers, and are famous preservers of good looks.

Charles Dickens

Christian love, either towards God or towards man, is an affair of the will.

C. S. Lewis

I preached as never sure to preach again; and as a dying man to dying men.

Richard Baxter, 1615–1691

<u>KEY</u>

Oddly, it is not real cooks who insist that the finest ingredients are necessary to produce a delicious something . . . Real cooks take stale bread and aging onions and make you happy.

Susan Wiegand, <u>Cooking as Courtship</u>

Be faithful in the little
practices of love which will
build in you the life of holiness
and make you Christlike.

"The Little Practices   Mother Teresa
of Love" — Aug. 10?

Good character is more to be
praised than outstanding
talent. Most talents are, to
some extent, a gift. Good
character, by contrast, is
not given to us. We have to
build it, piece by piece — by
thought, choice, courage and
determination.

                              H. Jackson Browne

Look round the habitable world; how few
know their own good, or know-
ing it, pursue.

John Dryden

Nothing that is worth doing
can be achieved in our lifetime;
therefore we must be saved by
hope. Nothing which is true
or beautiful or good makes
complete sense in any immediate
context of history; therefore
we must be saved by faith.
Nothing we do, however
virtuous, can be accomplished
alone; therefore, we must be
saved by love.

Reinhold Niebuhr

It takes a great man to make a good listener.

Arthur Helps

There are two things to aim at in life: first, to get what you want; and after that, to enjoy it. Only the wisest of mankind achieve the second.

—Logan Pearsall Smith, 1865–1946

Eat with the rich, but go play with the poor, who are capable of joy.

LPSmith, as above

Thank heavens, the sun has gone in, and I don't have to go out and enjoy it.

LP Smith

There are no uninteresting things, only uninterested people.

G K Chesterton

A thing long expected takes the form of the unexpected when at last it comes.

Mark Twain

Madeleine L'Engle calls the modern church "a safe place to escape the awful demands of God."

Also: "... we either add to the darkness of indifference ... or we light a candle to see by ..."

"Thy will be done" is what we're saying . . . We are askiing God to be God. We are asking God to do not only what we want but what God wants. we are askiing God to make manifest the holiness that is now mostly hidden, to set free in all its terrible splendor the devastating power that is now mostly under restraint . . .

"Thy kingdom come .. .on earth" is what we are saying. And iif that were suddenly to happen, what then? What would stand and what would fall? . . . To speak these words is to invite the tiger out of the cage. ..

You need to be bold in another way to speak the other half. Give us.

Forgive us. Don't test us.
Deliver us. If it takes guts
to face the omnipotence that iis
God's, it takes perhaps no less
to face the impotence that is
ours. We can do nothing without God. We can have nothing
without God. Without God we
are nothing.

It is only the words "Our
Father" whiich make the prayer
bearable. If God is indeed
something like a father, then
as somethiing like children
maybe we can risk approaching
him . . .

--Frederick Buechner, in
Listening to Your Life,
Daily Meditations with
Frederick Buechner

Those who bring sunshine to the lives of others cannot keep it from themselves.

James M. Barrie

There is something so indescribably sweet and satisfying in the knowledge that a husband or wife has forgiven the other freely, and from the heart.

Henrik Ibsen

There is no pillow so soft as a clear conscience.

French proverb

This is what marriage really means: helping one another to reach the full status of being persons, responsible beings who do not run away from life.

Paul Tournier

There are three stages in the work of God: impossible, difficult, done.

James Hudson Taylor,
English missionary

Surprise me, Lord, as a seed surprises itself . . .

George Herbert

Even a clock that doesn't work is right twice a day.

TV sermon

When you get in trouble for righteousness, God doesn't send somebody, He shows up Himself.

— TV sermon

Faith goes up the stairs that love has built and looks out the window which hope has opened.

Charles Spurgeon

Every saint has a past and every sinner has a future.

— 16th-century poet

Glorious truth

Reader! Had you in your mind
Such stores as silent thought
     can bring,
O gentle Reader! You would find
A tale in everything.
Wordsworth

John Muir argued that storms
of rain or snow were "a cordial
outpouring of Nature's love.
"How terribly downright," he
said, "must be the utterances of
storms and earthquakes to those
accustomed to the soft hypocrisies
of society."

A lie goes half way round the
world before the truth can get
its pants on.
Winston Churchill

Some are more concerned that
they be noticed than that
Christ might be seen.
                    Father Richard G. Bass

No disguise can long conceal
love where it exists, or long
feign it where it is lacking.
                    La Rochefoucauld

Anybody can sympathize
with the sufferings of a
friend, but it requires a very
fine nature to sympathize
with a friend's successes.
                    Oscar Wilde

Human felicity is produced
not so much by great pieces of
good fortune that seldom
happen, as by little advantages
that occur every day.

Benjamin Franklin

He has half the deed done who
has made a beginning.

Horace

Commit thy works unto the
Lord and thy thoughts shall
be established.

Proverbs 16:3

Whatever you would do, begin
it. Boldness has courage, genius
and magic in it.

Goethe

. . . she had long accepted the fact that happiness is like swallows iin spring. It may come and nest under your eaves or it may not. You cannot command iit. When you expect to be happy you are not, when you don't expect to be happy there is suddenly Easter in your soul, though it be midwinter. Something, you do not know what, has broken the seal upon that door in the depth of your being that opens upon eternity. It iis not yet timef for you yourself to go out of it but what is beyond comes in and passes into you and through you.

Elizabeth Goudge, <u>The White Witch</u>, copied from C's excerpt from the book

The reason lightning doesn't
strike twice in the same place is
that the same place isn't there
the second time.

Willie Tyler

WORD

I, who live by words, am
        wordless when
I try my words in prayer. All
        language turns
To silence. Prayer will take my words
        and then
Reveal their emptiness. The stifled voice
        learns
To hold its peace, to listen with the
        heart
To silence that is joy, is adoration.
The self is shattered, all words torn
        apart

In this strange patterned time of
    contemplation
That, in time, breaks time, breaks
    words, breaks me,
And then, in silence, leaves me
    healed and mended.
I have returned to language, for I see
Through words, even when all
    words are ended,
I, who live by words, am
    wordless when
I turn me to the Word to pray.
Amen.

—Madeleine L'Engle,
The Weather of the Heart

He who leaveth nothing to chance will do few things ill, but he will do very few things.

— George, Lord Halifax

My conviction is that we can say marvelous things without using a barbarous vocabulary.

Jean-Henri Fabre (1823–1915)

A little library, growing every year, is an honorable part of a man's history. It is a man's duty to have books.

Henry Ward Beecher

I cannot live without books.

Thos Jefferson

He who does not live in some
degree for others, hardly lives
for himself.

Montaigne

And none will hear the post-
man's knock without a
quickening of the heart. For
who can bear to feel himself
forgotten?

WH Auden, Night Mail

If you want to know your
true opinion of someone,
watch the effect produced in
you by the first sight of a
letter from him.

Schopenhauer

A writer lives in awe of words
for they can be cruel or kind,
and they can change their
meanings right in front of you.
They pick up flavors and odors
like butter in a refrigerator.

Anonymous

There are no words to express
the abyss between isolation and
having one ally. It may be
conceded to the mathematician
that four is twice two. But two
is not twice one; two is two
thousand times one.

GK Chesterton

An intention to write never turns into a letter. A letter must happen to one like a surprise, and one may not know where in the day there was room for it to come into being. So it is that my daily intentions have nothing to do with this fulfillment of today.

Rainer Maria Rilke

Asked to write a letter to the London Times on "What's wrong with the world?" GK Chesterton wrote, "Dear Sirs, I am.
Yours truly, GK Chesterton."

Peter Kreeft

Write to me often. Write
affectionately, and freely, as
I do to you. Say many kind
things, and say them without
reserve. They will be food for
my soul.

      Thos Jefferson to Maria Cosway

Preserve for me always a little
corner in your affection in
exchange for the spacious part
you occupy in mine. Adieu ma
chere et tres chere amie!

      Thos Jeff to M. Cosway

. . . remember me and love me.

      TJ to MC

A great deal of love given to a few is better than a little to many.

Thos Jefferson

God is not morally neutral.

Francis Schaeffer

The Bible is the chief moral cause of all that is good, and the best book for regulating the concerns of men . . . The man, therefore, who weakens or destroys the divine authority of that book may be accessory to all the public disorders which society is doomed to suffer.

Peter Marshall, 1902—1949

God does not care . . . whether I am
happy or not. What God cares about,
with all the power of God's holy being,
iis the quality of my life. . .not just
the continuation of my breath and the
health of my cells--but the quality of
my life, the scope of my life, the heft
and zest of my life . . .fear of death
always turns into fear of life, iinto a
stingy, cautious way of living that is
not really living at all . . . to follow
Jesus means going beyond the limits of
our own comfort and safety. It means
receiving our lives as gifts iinstead of
guarding them as . . . possessions.

Rev. Barbara Brown Taylor

Accept, O Lord, my entire liberty, my memory, my understanding, and my will. All that I am and have thou hast given to me; and I give all back to thee to be disposed of according to thy good pleasure. Give me only the comfort of thy presence and the joy of thy love; with thee I shall be more than rich and shall desire nothing more.

St. Ignatius of Loyola

I know the plans I have for you, says the Lord. They are plans for good and not for evil, to give you a future and a hope.

Jeremiah 29:11 (which translation?)

Last Words:

Now comes the mystery.

Henry Ward Beecher

Into thy hands, O Lord,
I commend my spirit.

Christopher Columbus

It is very beautiful over there.

Thomas Edison

Is this dying? Is this all? Is
this what I feared when I
prayed against a hard death?
Oh, I can bear this! I can
bear it!

Cotton Mather

This isn't bad. Tell everyone
this really isn't bad at all . . .
it's beautiful out there!

Stephen Foster

*

The marvelous richness of human experience would lose something of rewarding joy if there were not limitations to overcome. The hilltop would not be half so wonderful if there were no dark valleys to traverse.

Helen Keller

The greater the obstacle, the more glory in overcoming it.

Molière

I can do all things through Christ who strengthens me.

Philippians 4:13

From every cut springs new growth.

Source unknown

You must find a way or make one.

Hannibal

Trifles make perfection, and perfection is no trifle.

Michelangelo

There's no limit to what can be accomplished if it doesn't matter who gets the credit.

— don't know who said this

Be of good cheer.

A commandment!   Matt. 14:27

The best thing about the
future is that it comes only
one day at a time.
                        Abraham Lincoln

Lord, purge our eyes to see
Within the seed a tree
Within the glowing egg a bird,
Within the shroud a butterfly.
Till, taught by such we see
Beyond all creatures, Thee . . .

                        Christina Rossetti

In the name of Jesus Christ, who was never in a hurry, we pray, O God, that You will slow us down, for we know that we live too fast. With all of eternity before us, make us take time to live— time to get acquainted with You, time to enjoy Your blessings, and time to know each other.

—Peter Marshall, 1902–1949

Love wholeheartedly, be surprised, give thanks and praise. Then you will discover the fullness of your life.

Brother David Steindl-Rast

O God, Light of lights
Keep us from inward darkness
Grant us so to sleep in peace,
that we may arise to work
        according
to Your Will.
        — Lancelot Andrewes, 1555–1626

When you reread a classic,
you do not see more in the
book than you did before; you
see more in yourself than there
was before.
        Clifton Fadiman

Opportunity is missed by most
people because it is dressed in
overalls and looks like work.
        Thomas Edison

Those who wish to succeed
must ask the right preliminary
questions.

Aristotle, _Metaphysics_, II

Those who make religion their
god will not have God for
their religion.

Thomas Erskine of Linlathen

You can say any foolish
thing to a dog, and the dog
will give you a look that says,
"...you're right! I never
would've thought of that!"

—Dave Barry

Upon thy bended knees,
thank God for work,
Work— once man's penance,
now his high reward!
For work to do,
and strength
to do the work,
We thank Thee, Lord!

—John Oxenham, 1861?—1941
Was William Dunkerley, novelist,
poet, hymnist, e.g., "In Christ
There Is No East or West"

We live as those who are on a journey home: a home we know will have the lights on and the door open and our father waiting for us when we arrive. That means in all adversity our worship of God is joyful, our life is hopeful, our future is secure. There is nothing we can lose on earth that can rob us of the treasures God has given us and will give us.

ibid.

On character:

Loose translation of Emerson: Character is like an acrostic or Alexandrian stanza: read it forward, backward, or across, it will spell the same thing.

Dwight Moody: Character is what you are in the dark.

Lord Macaulay: The measure of a man's real character is what he would do if he knew he would never be found out.

Shakespeare: The best men are often molded out of faults.

Charles Reade: Sow an act, and you reap a habit. Sow a habit and you reap a character. Sow a character and you reap a destiny.

Helen Keller: Character cannot be developed in ease and quiet. Only through experience of trial and suffering can the soul be strengthened; vision cleared; ambition inspired, and success achieved.

Sir J. Stevens: Every one of us has in himself a continent of undiscovered character. Happy is he who acts the Columbus to his own soul.

Man's extremity is God's
opportunity.

John Flavel, English
Presbyterian minister, d. 1691

Praise makes good men better
and bad men worse.

Thomas Fuller, 1608—1661

Prayer . . . the key of the day
and the lock of the night.

Thos Fuller

When I was threatening to become cold
in my ministry, and when I felt
Sabbath morning coming, and my heart
not filled wiith amazement at the
grace of God, or when I was makiing
ready to dispense the Lord's
Supper . . . I used to take a turn up
and down among the sins of my past
life, and I I always came down with a
broken and a contrite heart, ready to
preach . . . the forgiveness of sins.

Thos Goodwin, English Puritan minister, 1600-1680

A man who cannot find
tranquility within himself will
search for it in vain elsewhere.

François, Duc de La Rochefoucauld,
French writer, 1613–1680

Amen

Gather ye rosebuds while ye may,
Old Time is still a-flying.

Robt Herrick, Church of England
clergyman, poet, 1591–1674

Here a little child I stand,
Heaving up my either hand;
Cold as paddocks though they be,
Here I lift them up to thee,
For a benison to fall
On our meat, and on us all.

Herrick

Cold as paddocks! yes, too often

Let us weigh the gain and the loss, in wagering that God is. Consider these alternatives: if you win, you win all, if you lose you lose nothing. Do not hesitate, then, to wager that he is.

Blaise Pascal, Fr. mathematician, physicist, theologian, man of letters, 1623—1662

Grace is indeed needed to turn a man into a saint, and he who doubts it does not know what a saint or a man is.

Pascal

Be careful to preserve your health. It is a trick of the devil, which he employs to deceive good souls, to incite them to do more than they are able, in order that they may no longer be able to do anything.

Amen and amen!

Vincent de Paul, Fr Roman Catholic priest, 1581—1660

Hear this, Timothy, hear this!

Whenever I find myself in the cellar of affliction, I always look about for the wine.

Samuel Rutherford, 1600s, Scottish minister

And this:

Jesus Christ came into my
prison cell last night, and
every stone flashed like a ruby.

Also from Rutherford

Grace grows better in the winter.

Fine fellow, read him again
and again

I am never better than when
I am on the full stretch
for God.

Geo. Whitefield

The full stretch! May it be so!

A man of quality is never threatened by a woman of equality.

Jill Briscoe, English Bible teacher, writer

Never say that you have no time. On the whole it is those who are busiest who can make time for yet more, and those who have more leisure time who refuse to do something when asked. What we lack is not time, but heart.

Henri Boulard, Egyptian Jesuit

Quietude, which some men cannot abide because it reveals their inward poverty, is as a palace of cedar to the wise, for along its hallowed courts the King in his beauty deigns to walk.

Charles Haddon Spurgeon, 1834—1892

The worst thing that can happen to a man who gambles is to win.

CHS

There are some things that can be learned by the head, but... Christ crucified can only be learned by the heart.

CHS

It is a wonderful accomplishment and a most bountiful answer to one's prayers, to have obtained a wife in the highest matters and the smallest details after my imagination and my heart.

Anthony Ashley Cooper, Earl of Shaftesbury, 1801–1885

A real Christian is the one who can give his pet parrot to the town gossip.

Billy Graham

It is unnatural for Christianity to be popular.

B. Graham

Nobody worries about Christ
as long as he can be kept
shut up in churches. He is
quite safe inside. But there is
always trouble if you try and
let him out.

Geoffrey A. Studdert-Kennedy,
1883–1929, chaplain WWI

Prayer must carry on our
work as much as preaching;
he preacheth not heartily to
his people, that will not pray
for them.

Richard Baxter, 1615–1691

Be great in little things.

Francis Xavier (1506–1552),
Jesuit teacher, missionary

Help me this day to live a
simple, sincere and serene
life, repelling promptly
every thought of discontent,
anxiety, discouragement, im-
purity, and self-seeking;
cultivating cheerfulness,
magnanimity, charity, and the
habit of holy siilence; exer-
cising economy in expenditure,
generosity iin giving, careful-
ness in conversation, diligence
in appointed service, fidelity
to every trust, and a childlike
faith in God.

In particular I will try to be
faithful in those habits of
prayer, work, study, physical
exercise, eatiing and sleep
which I believe the Holy ~~Sprit~~
Spirit has shown me to be right.

And as I cannot in my own
strength do thiis, nor even with
a hope of success attempt it,
I look to thee, O Lord God my
Father, iin Jesus my Savior,
and ask for the gift of the
Holy Spirit.

From <u>Forward Day by Day</u>

It is the great curse of Gluttony
that it ends by destroying all
sense of the precious, the unique,
the irreplaceable.

Dorothy Sayers

(When) Jesus Himself fasted,
He was not fasting to repent
or to bring His desires under
control, of course, but to
demonstrate His absolute
dependence upon His Father.

Peter C. Moore, Trinity Seminary

Almighty and eternal God, so draw my heart to You, so guide my mind, so fill my imagination, so control my will, that I may be wholly Yours, utterly dedicated unto You; and then use me, I pray, as You will, and always to Your glory, and the welfare of Your people; through our Lord and Savior Jesus Christ. Amen.

Source unknown

By words the mind is winged.

Aristophanes

A something in your eyes, and
voice, you possess in a degree
more persuasive than any
woman I ever saw, read, or
heard of . . . that bewitching
sort of nameless excellence.

Laurence Sterne
to Eliza Draper, 1762

I have told my passion, my
eyes have spoke it, my tongue
pronounced it, and my pen
declared it . . . Now my heart
is full of you, my head raves
of you, and my hand writes
to you . . .

George Farquhar to Anne Oldfield,
1700

It is not in my power to tell
thee how I have been affected
by thiis dearest of all letters--
it was so unexpected--so new a
thing to see the breathing of
thy inmost heart upon paper
that I was quite overpowered,
& now that I sit down to answer thee in the loneliness &
Depth of that love which
unites us & which cannot be
felt but by ourselves, I am so
agitated & My eyes are so
bedimmed that I scarcely know
how to proceed . . .

      Mary Wordsworth to her husband
      William, 1810

Don't write too legibly or intelligibly as I have no occupation so pleasant as pondering for hours over your hieroglyphics, and for hours more trying to interpret your . . . sayings. A clearly written simply expressed letter is too like the lightning.

—Duff Cooper to his future wife, 1914

D. Cooper the finest of
ltr. writers

All my soul follows you, love . . . and I live in being yours.

Robert Browning to E. Barrett, 1846

I can neither eat nor sleep for thinking of You my dearest love, I never touch even pudding.

Horatio Nelson to
Lady Emma Hamilton, 1800

Of course, you haven't got to decide, but think about it. I can't advise you in my favour because I think it would be beastly for you, but think how nice it would be for me!

Evelyn Waugh proposing to
Laura Herbert, 1936

If two people who
love each other
let a single instant
wedge itself between
them, it grows —
it becomes a month,
a year, a century;
it becomes too late.
— Jean Giraudoux

I swear to you were we not married I would beg you on my knees to be my wife, which I could not do did I not esteem you as well as I love you.

John Churchill to Sarah, his wife, 1680

Nothing new here, except my marrying, which to me is a matter of profound wonder.

Abraham Lincoln of his marriage to M. Todd, 1842

The nomad spirit of modernity has dashed the integrity of community—but not the deep need for it.

Harold Beekser, 1922–1997

Work is much more fun
than fun.

Noël Coward, 1899—1973

A wise man will make
more opportunities than
he finds.

Francis Bacon, 1561—1626

If your ship doesn't
come in, swim out to it.

Andy Tant

My son, ill-gotten gains do not profit,
but righteousness delivers from
death. The Lord will not allow the
righteous to hunger, but He will
thrust aside the craving of the
wicked. Poor ishe who works with a
negligent hand, but the hand of the
diligent makes rich. The soul of the
sluggard craves and gets nothing, but
the soul of the diligent is made
fat. Wealth obtained by fraud dwin-
dles, but the one who gathers by
labor increases it. A man can do
nothing better than fiind satisfaction
iin his work.

King Solomon, c. 1000Ø B.C.

Commend me to sterling
honesty, though clad in rags.
Sir Walter Scott, 1771—1832

We trust, not because a God
exists, but because this God
exists.
CS Lewis, 1898—1963

Man is
what
he believes.
Chekhov, 1860—
1904

When you carry out acts of kindness, you get a wonderful feeling inside. It is as though something inside your body responds and says, "Yes, this is how I ought to feel."

— Rabbi Harold Kushner

Sermon, 8/14
It is crucial that we allow others to show kindness to us.

To be happy at home is the end of all labor.

Samuel Johnson, 1709–1784

The future is purchased at the price of vision in the present.

Saml Johnson

Understanding is knowing
what to do; wisdom is
knowing what to do next;
virtue is actually doing it.

Tristan Gylberd, 1954—

What you do when you don't
have to, determines what you
will be when you can no
longer help it.

Rudyard Kipling, 1865—1936

A lie stands on one leg, the
truth on two.

B. Franklin

I love the smell of book ink in
the morning.

Umberto Eco, 1929–

The honest man takes pains,
and then enjoys pleasures, the
knave takes pleasure and then
suffers pain.

B franklin, 1706–1790

The idle man does not know
what it is to enjoy rest.

Albert Einstein, 1879–1955

When we have accepted the worst, we have nothing more to lose. And that automatically means we have everything to gain.

— Dale Carnegie

We are perpetually being told that what is wanted is a strong man who will do things. What is really wanted is a strong man who will undo things; and that will be the real test of strength.

G. K. Chesterton, 1874—1936

If you cannot read all your books, at any rate . . . peer into them, let them fall open where they will, read from the first sentence that arrests the eye, set them back on the shelves with your own hands, arrange them on your own plan so that you at least know where they are. Let them be your friends; let them be your acquaintances.

Winston Churchill, 1874—1965

Education is not the filling of a pail but the lighting of a fire.

William Butler Yeats, 1865—1939

Where is human nature so weak as in the bookstore?

Henry Ward Beecher, 1813—1887

where, indeed?!!!

Great tranquility of heart is his who cares for neither praise nor blame.

Thomas à Kempis

The world does not need more Christian writers— it needs more good writers and composers who are Christians.

C. S. Lewis

The most extraordinary thing
in the world is an ordinary
man and an ordinary
woman and their ordinary
children.

G. K. Chesterton

I am of certain convinced
that the greatest heroes are
those who do their duty in
the daily grind of domestic
affairs whilst the world
whirls as a maddening
dreidel.

Florence Nightingale, 1820—1910

I find in myself a desire which no experience in this world can satisfy, the most profitable explanation is that I was made for another world.

C. S. Lewis

One does not discover new lands without consenting to lose sight of the shore.

André Gide, 1869—1951
Amen!

Live deep instead of fast.

Henry Seidel Canby

The older theology tended to
produce character. By the end of
the twentiieth century, we have
become God's demanding little
brats. In church, we must be
entertained. Our emotions must
be charged. We must be offered
amusing programs. We give up a
lot to become Christians and
what little teaching we do get
must cater to our pbagmatic,
self-centered interests.
Preaching must be filled wiith
clever anecdotes and colorful
illustrations with nothing more
than passing references to doc-
trine. I want to know what this
means for me in my daily experience. Have we forgotten that
God is a monarch? He is the king,
by whom and for whom all things
were made and by whose sovereign
power they are sustained. We
exist for hiis pleasure, not he
for ours. We are on this earth
to entertain him, please him,
adore him, bring hiim satisfaction, excitement and joy. Any
gospel that seeks to answer the
question, "What's in this for
me?" has iit all backwards.
The question is, "What's in
it for God?"

                    --Mike Horton

He is not great who is not
greatly good.

—Shakespeare

None are so old as those who
have outlived enthusiasm.

—Henry Thoreau, 1817—1862

Love must be as much a
light, as it is a flame.

—Thoreau

It is better to have traveled
and gotten lost than to never
have traveled at all.

— Geo. Santayana, 1863–1952

Traveling abroad is a progressive
exercise in the discovery of our
own ignorance.

— Wm Blake, 1757–1827

I hope I shall always possess
firmness and virtue enough to
maintain what I consider the
most enviable of all titles, the
character of an honest man.

— Geo Washington, 1732–1799

The enemies of the truth are always awfully nice.

—Christopher Morley, 1890–1957

The streets of hell are paved with good intentions.

—Twain

Those who are quick to promise are generally slow to perform. They promise mountains and perform molehills.

—Spurgeon, 1834–1892

To know that which before us
lies in daily life is the prime
wisdom.
— Milton

The wise does at once what
the fool does at last.
— Baltasar Gracián, 1601–1658

The fear of the Lord is the
beginning of wisdom . . .
Solomon

If you have a job without
aggravation, you don't have
a job.
— Malcolm Forbes, 1919–1990

The world does not consider
labor a blessing, therefore it flees
and hates it, but the pious
who fear the Lord labor with
a ready and cheerful heart,
for they know God's command
and will, they acknowledge His
calling.

— Martin Luther, 1483–1546

Genius is seldom recognized
for what it is: a great capacity
for hard work.

— Henry Ford, 1863–1947

The Bible will keep you from
sin, or sin will keep you from
the Bible.

D L Moody, 1837–1899

As high as we have mounted in
    delight,
In our dejection do we sink as low.

Wm Wordsworth

Unless we form the habit of
going to the Bible in bright
moments as well as in trouble,
we cannot fully respond to its
consolations because we lack
equilibrium between light and
darkness.

Helen Keller

If you believe what you like in
the gospels, and reject what
you don't like, it is not the
gospel you believe, but yourself.

St. Augustine

One man with courage makes
a majority.
            Andrew Jackson, 1767—1845

O. Holy Spirit, descend plentifully
into my heart. Enlighten the
dark corners of this neglected
dwelling and scatter there Thy
cheerful beams.
                        St. Augustine

To have what we want is
riches, but to be able to do
without is power.
                    Geo Macdonald

Indeed, I tremble for my
country when I reflect that
God is just.

Thos Jefferson

Our birth is but a sleep and a
      forgetting;
The soul that rises with us,
      our life's star,
Hath had elsewhere its setting,
And cometh from afar.
Not in entire forgetfulness,
And not in utter nakedness,
But trailing clouds of glory,
      do we come
From God, who is our home.

Wordsworth

Trailing clouds of glory!!

It is a bad world, Donatus, an
incredibly bad world. But I have dis-
covered iin the midst of it a quiet
and good people who have learned the
great secret of life. They have found
a joy and a wisdom whiich is a thousand times better than any of the
pleasures of our sinful life. They
are despised and persecuted, but they
care not. They are masters of their
  souls. They have overcome the world.
These people, Donatus, are Christians . . . andI am one of them.

st. Cyprian, 200-258

Mark This!

You cannot do a kindness too soon, for you never know how soon it will be too late.

Emerson

Noah was a brave man to sail in a wooden boat with two termites.

Anon.

The man who covets is always poor.

Claudian, c. 370–c. 404

It is a characteristic of wisdom not to do desperate things.

Thoreau

Why don't you get a haircut?
You look like a chrysanthemum.

   P. G. Wodehouse, 1881—1975

  Is this Cyn. or Wodehouse?

Man is certainly stark mad.
He cannot make a worm and
yet he will be making gods by
the dozens.

    Montaigne, 1533—1592

Dare to be honest and fear
no labor.

    Robt Burns, 1759—96

Letter writing is the only device for combining solitude with good company.

Lord Byron, 1788–1824

Preach the gospel all the time. If necessary, use words.

St. Francis

It is impossible to enjoy idling unless there is plenty of work to do.

Jerome K. Jerome, 1859–1927

If you take too long in deciding
what to do with your life,
you'll find you've done it.

Geo. B. Shaw, 1856–1950

A loving person lives in a
loving world. A hostile person
lives in a hostile world;
everyone you meet is your
mirror.

Ken Keyes, Jr., 1921–1990

The devil will let a preacher
prepare a sermon if it will keep
him from preparing himself.

Vance Havner

The lowest ebb is the turn of the tide.

Longfellow, 1807–1882

Lord, grant that I may always desire more than I can accomplish.

Michelangelo, 1475–1564

We have all eternity to celebrate our victories, but only one short hour before sunset in which to win them.

Robt Moffat, 1795–1883

What we need is not the old acceptance of the world as a compromise,
but some ʂway in whiich we can heartily hate and heartily love iit. We do
not want joy and anger to neutralize
each other and produce a surly contentment; we want a fiercer delight
and fiercer discontent. We have to
see the universe at once as an
ogreʂs castle, to be stormed, and yet
as our own cottage, to which we can
return at eveniing.

G. K. Chesterton, 1874-1936

Strong stuff

Love so amazing, so divine,
demands my soul, my life,
my all.

Isaac Watts, 1674—1748

If there's a job to be done, I
always ask the busiest men in
my parish to take it on and
it gets done.

Henry Ward Beecher, 1813—1887

Courage is what it takes to
stand up and speak; courage
is also what it takes to sit
down and listen.

Churchill

Though we travel the world over to find the beautiful, we must carry it with us or we find it not.

Emerson

That which is striking and beautiful is not always good, but that which is good is always beautiful.

Ninon de Lenclos

We are always getting ready to live, but never living.

Emerson

The heights by great men reached
and kept
Were not attained by sudden flight,
But they, while their companions
slept,
Were toiling upward in the night.

Longfellow

Where courage is not, no other
virtue can survive except by
accident.

Samuel Johnson, 1709—1784

The difference between the right
word and the almost right word
is like the difference between
lightning and the lightning bug.

Twain

The wicked flee when no one
pursues, but the righteous are
bold as a lion.   This
                    Solomon

Far better it is to dare mighty
things, to win glorious triumphs,
even though checkered by failure,
than to take rank with those
poor spirits who neither enjoy
much nor suffer much because
they live in the gray twilight
that knows neither victory
nor defeat.
                    Theo. Roosevelt, 1858—1919

This

For God has not given us a
spirit of fear, but of power
and of love and of a sound
mind.

St. Paul

A bold Christian is the highest
style of a man.

Thos Young

I believe in Christianity as I
believe that the sun has risen
not only because I see it, but
because by it I see everything else.

—C. S. Lewis

If we really think that home
is elsewhere, and that this life
is a "wandering to find home,"
why should we not look
forward to the arrival?

Lewis

But suddenly what had been
an ideal had become a
demand—total surrender to
God, the absolute leap in the
dark, the demand was not
"all or nothing," that stage
had been passed. Now the
demand was simply "all!"

Lewis

Once a man is united to God
how could he not live forever?
Once a man is separated from
God, what can he do but
wither and die?

Lewis

This habit of reading, I make
bold to tell you, is your pass
to the greatest, the purest, and
the most perfect pleasure that
God has prepared for His
creatures. It lasts when all
other pleasures fade. It will
support you when all other
recreations are gone. It will
last until your death. It will
make your hours pleasant to
you as long as you live.

Anthony Trollope, 1815–1882

. . . it is very well worthwhile
to be tormented for two or
three years of one's life, for
the sake of being able to read
all the rest of it.

Jane Austen, 1775–1817

Read at every wait; read at all
hours; read within leisure; read
in times of labor; read as one
goes in; read as one goes out.
The task of the educated mind
is simply put: read to lead.

Cicero, 106–43 B.C.

You can't get a cup of tea
large enough or a book long
enough to suit me.

Lewis

Books are not dead things, but do contain a potency of life ... as active as that soul was whose progeny they are; nay, they do preserve as in a vial the purest extraction of that living intellect that bred them.

John Milton, 1608—1674

It is a good plan to have a book with you in all places and at all times. If you are presently without, hurry without delay to the nearest shop and buy one of mine.

O. Wendell Holmes, 1809—1894

Prayer is either a sheer illusion or
a personal contact between embryonic,
incomplete persons (ourselves) and
the utterly concrete Person. Prayer
in the sense of petition, asking
for things, is a small part of iit
confession and penitance are its
threshold, adoration its sanctuary,
the presence and vision and enjoy-
ment of God its bread and wine. In
it God shows himself to us. That
He answers prayer is a corollary,
not necessarily the most important
one, from that revelation. What
He does is learned from what He
is.
C. S. Lewis, "The Efficacy of
Prayer," from <u>The World's Last</u>
<u>Night</u> <u>and</u> <u>Other</u> <u>Essays</u>, 1959

We make our friends, we make
our enemies, but God makes
our next-door neighbor.

GK Chesterton, 1874 – 1936

Poets have been mysteriously
quiet on the subject of cheese.

Chesterton

Life is not so short but
that there is always time
for courtesy and chivalry.

Emerson

Amor vincit omnia.

Chaucer, 1342—1400

If you have an important
point to make, don't try to be
subtle or clever. Use the pile
driver. Hit the point once.
Then come back and hit
it again. Then hit it a
third time; a tremendous
whack.

Churchill

Send to
Stuart

Man will occasionally stumble
over the truth, but most of
the time he will pick himself
up and continue on.

Churchill

...I remember the story of the old man who said on his deathbed that he had had a lot of trouble in his life, most of which had never happened.

Churchill

One ought never to turn one's back on a threatened danger and try to run away from it. If you do that, you will double the danger. But if you meet it promptly and without flinching, you will reduce the danger by half. Never run away from anything. Never!

Churchill

Courage is not having the
strength to go on; it is going
on when you don't have
the strength. Industry and
determination can do anything
that genius and advantage
can do and many things
that they cannot.

Theodore Roosevelt, 1858—1919

Understanding is the reward
of faith. Therefore seek not to
understand that you may
believe, but believe that you
may understand.

St. Augustine

Prov. 16:22
15:32
14:29
Prov. 24:3

The Christian faith has not
been tried and found wanting.
It has been found difficult,
and left untried.

Chesterton

He is your friend who pushes
you nearer to God.

Abraham Kuyper, 1837 — 1920

He speaketh not;
And yet there lies
A conversation
In his eyes.

Longfellow

When two go together, one of them at least looks forward to see what is best; a man by himself, though he be careful, still has less mind in him than two, and his wits have less weight.

Homer, c. 900 B.C.

Sept. 7, one flesh

Real friendship is shown in times of trouble; prosperity is full of friends.

A. Kuyper

Oh, the comfort, the inexpressible comfort of feeling safe with a person: having neither to weigh thoughts nor measure words, but to pour them out. Just as they are — chaff and grain together, knowing that a faithful hand will take and sift them, keep what is worth keeping, and then with the breath of kindness, blow the rest away.

Geo Eliot, 1819—1880

If you have a friend worth
        loving,
    Love him. Yes, and let him
        know
That you love him, ere life's
        evening
    Tinge his brow with sunset
        glow.
Why should good words ne'er
        be said
Of a friend—till he is dead?

        Alexander MacLeod, 1786–1869

It may be true that he travels
farthest who travels alone,
but the goal thus reached is
not worth reaching.

        T. Roosevelt

Friendship doubles our joys
and halves our grief.

Dolley Madison, 1768—1849

A merry heart doeth good like
a medicine.

Proverbs 17:22

Friendships, like geraniums,
bloom in kitchens.

Peter Lorimer, 1812—1879

Be courteous to all, but intimate
with few, and let those few be
well tried before you give them
your confidence. True friendship
is a plant of slow growth,
and must undergo and with-
stand the shocks of adversity
before it is entitled to the
appellation.

Geo Washington

All heaven and earth resound
with that subtle and delicately
balanced truth that the
old paths are the best paths
after all.

J. C. Ryle, 1816—1900

Any woodsman can tell
you that in a broken and
sundered nest, one can hardly
expect to find more than a
precious few whole eggs. So
it is with the family.

                    Thos Jefferson

The family is the true society.
                    Pope Leo XIII, 1810—1903

The chains of habit are too
weak to be felt until they are
too strong to be broken.

                    Samuel Johnson, 1709—1784

"We are fools for Christ's
sake," Paul says in the first
letter to the Corinthians. God
is foolish, too, Paul says. God
iis foolish to choose for his
holy work iin the world the kind
of lamebrains and misfits and
nit-pickers and odd ducks and
stuffed shirts and egomaniacs
and milquetoasts and closet
sensualists as are vividly
represented by us all.
    God is foolish to send usout
to speak hope to a world that
slogs along heart-deep in
the conviction that things can
only get worse . . . He is
foolish to have us speak of
loving our enemies when we have
a hard enough time loving our
friends . . . God is foolish to
have us proclaim eternal life
to a world that is half in
love wiith death . . . God is
foolish to send us out on a
journey for which there are no
maps, and to aim us in the dir-
ection of a goal we can never
know until we get there. Such
is the foolishness of God.
And yet, and yet, Paul says,
"the foolishness of God is
wiser ¢than man."

        --Frederick Buechner

But words are things, and a
small drop of ink, falling like
dew upon a thought, produces
that which makes thousands,
perhaps millions, think.

Lord Byron, 1788—1824

Lay hold of something that
will help you, and then use it
to help somebody else.

Booker T. Washington, 1856—1915

Mercy has converted more
souls than zeal, or eloquence,
or learning or all of them
together.

Søren Kierkegaard, 1813—1855

The ultimate effect of our mass cul-
ture is to make children older than
their years, to turn them iinto the
knowing, cynical pseudo-adult that is
by now the model kid of the TV sit-
com. It iis a crime against children
to make them older than their years.
And it won't do for the purveyors of
cynicism to hide behiind the First
Amendment. Of course they have the
right to publish and peddle thiis
trash to kids. But they should have
the decency ℓ∅not to. Let us therefore
take a pledge, a stand, a covenant,
against such rubbish, and recommit
ourselves to the great civilizing
impulse that gave rise to such things
as libraries.

    Charles Krauthammer, 1939 -

How easy is it for one benevolent being to diffuse pleasure around him, and how truly is a kind heart a fountain of gladness, making everything in its vicinity to freshen into smiles.

Washington Irving, 1783—1859

Where there are no good works, there is no faith. If works and love do not blossom forth, it is not genuine faith, the Gospel has not yet gained a foothold, and Christ is not yet rightly known.

Martin Luther, 1483—1546

Mercy is the golden chain by
which society is bound together.

Wm Blake, 1757—1827

We do not need to get good laws
to restrain bad people. We need to
get good people to restrain bad
laws.

Chesterton

There is no trick being a
humorist when you have the
whole government working for you.

Will Rogers

The hardest thing in the
world to understand is the
income tax.

Albert Einstein

If men will not be governed by
the Ten Commandments they
shall be governed by the ten
thousand commandments.

Chesterton

It is impossible to mentally or
socially enslave a Bible-reading
people.

Horace Greeley

A billion here, a billion there;
the first thing you know,
you're talking about real
money.

Everett Dirksen

The world has always been betrayed by decent men with bad ideals.

Sydney J. Harris

The philosophy of the classroom in one generation will be the philosophy of government in the next.

Abraham Lincoln

In literature as in love, courage is half the battle.

Sir Walter Scott, 1771—1832

I sought for the greatness and genius
of America in her commodious harbors
and her ample rivers, and iit was not
there; in her fertile fields and
boundless prairies, and it was not
there; in her rich mines and her
vast world commerce, and iit was not
there. Not until I went to the
churches of America and heard her
pulpits aflame with righteousness did
I understand the secret of her genius
and power. America is great because
she is good and iif America ever
ceases to be good, America will cease
to be great.

Alexis de Tocqueville, 1805-1859

And now in age I bud again
After so many deaths I live and
     write
I once more smell the dew and rain
And relish versing: O my only Light
It cannot be
That I am he
On whom Thy tempests fell all night.
          —George Herbert

Know that there is often hidden
in us a dormant poet, always
young and alive.
          de Musset

Is death the last step? No, it
is the final awakening.
          Scott

Ps. 27:14   Isaiah 25:6

27:5   25:10

28:7   26:3 THIS

31:3
        39:20-21

32:8   40:29

34:4   41:10

34:18   42:16

37:3-5

37:25   Joel 2:25

40:8   And I will

46:1-3 restore to you

48:14   the years that

51:10   the locust

55:22   hath eaten...

62:6   (Pauline) Buck, also

62:12

64:10   Romans 9:10

Eccl. 9:9

9:10

I have come home

If any thing delight me for to print
My book, 'tis this; that thou, my
            God,
art in 't.

Robert Herrick, Church of England
        clergyman, poet, 1591–1674

Father Timothy Andrew Kavanagh is the principal character in author Jan Karon's series of bestselling Mitford novels, set in a mountain village in western North Carolina. Father Tim is a sixtysomething Episcopal priest beloved by parishioners for his unfailing concern for their needs, and for his exceptional warmth, grace, charm, and devotion to God.

In this book, Father Tim has recorded favorite quotes from a variety of thinkers, philosophers, and poets who have enlisted his admiration over the years.

Thanks to: Fr. Nick Minich; *The Christian Quotation Collection*, Lion Publishing, England; *Love Letters, An Anthology of Passion*, Michelle Lovric, Marlowe & Co.; *The Christian Almanac: A Dictionary of Days Celebrating History's Most Significant People and Events*, by George Grant & Gregory Wilbur; *The Address Book*, Michael Levine, Putnam; *Bartlett's Book of Quotations*, without which we should all be adither; *The Blowing Rocket*, which regularly publishes pithy quotes; and to various other sources throughout the years, from wayside pulpits to the peripatetic Anon.

Special thanks to: Dr. George Grant, author, teacher, philosopher, friend.

OTHER MITFORD BOOKS BY JAN KARON

At Home in Mitford

A Light in the Window

These High, Green Hills

Out to Canaan

A New Song

A Common Life

The Mitford Snowmen

CHILDREN'S BOOKS

Miss Fannie's Hat

Jeremy: The Tale of an Honest Bunny

Coming in 2002:

In This Mountain,

the seventh novel in Jan Karon's bestselling
Mitford Years series.

VIKING

Published by the Penguin Group
Penguin Putnam Inc., 375 Hudson Street,
New York, New York 10014, U.S.A.
Penguin Books Ltd, 27 Wrights Lane, London W8 5TZ, England
Penguin Books Australia Ltd, Ringwood, Victoria, Australia
Penguin Books Canada Ltd, 10 Alcorn Avenue,
Toronto, Ontario, Canada M4V 3B2
Penguin Books (N.Z.) Ltd, 182-190 Wairau Road,
Auckland 10, New Zealand

Penguin Books Ltd, Registered Offices:
Harmondsworth, Middlesex, England

First published in 2001 by Viking Penguin,
a member of Penguin Putnam Inc.

1 3 5 7 9 10 8 6 4 2

Pages 191–192 constitute an extension of this copyright page.

LIBRARY OF CONGRESS CATALOGING IN PUBLICATION DATA
Patches of godlight: Father Tim's favorite quotes.
p. cm.—(The seventh volume in the beloved Mitford series by Jan Karon)
ISBN 0-670-03006-6
1. Quotations, English.
PN6081 .P44 2001
082—dc21   2001017746

This book is printed on acid-free paper.

∞

Printed in the United States of America
Designed by Francesca Belanger and Glenn Timony